I0640943

Firebrand Firestorm

The Ancestors of Bjorn Esterday

Volume 07

Secrets

June 1776

Wynter Sommers

Wynter Sommers

This work is registered with the UK Copyright Service, in
accordance with the Copyright, Designs and Patents Act 1988
All rights reserved 284718040

USA Copyright © 2015 GJ dePillis
© 2015, TXu001966602 / 2015-05-08 and TXu001983965 / 2015-11-04

Library of Congress Control Number: 2020943167

Published by Pure Force Enterprises, Inc.
California, USA
Since 2002

INGRAM

INGRAM® Distribution

ISBN-13: 978-1-7184-0019-1
ISBN-10: 1-7184-0019-5

DEDICATION

To those who feel strongly about truth, justice, and the integrity of America; your honorable actions make us proud. To those who wonder if their daily choices matter; your small decisions impact generations to come.To those everyday people who don't think they have what it takes; when you strive for extraordinary things, the impossible becomes reality.Your dreams today become our future tomorrow.Thank you for everything you do.

Bjorn Esterday
Was Not Born Yesterday
Series

Firebrand (15 Volumes+Conversation Station Book)
Edges (9 Stories +Conversation Station Book)
Gone (18 Stories + Conversation Station Book)

Bjorn EDGES Series
EDGES Book 1-Swift Encounter
EDGES Book 2-Rousing Attack
EDGES Book 3-One Foot Under
EDGES Book 4-Earthshake
EDGES Book 5-Broken String
EDGES Book 6-Key Witness
EDGES Book 7-Who is She?
EDGES Book 8-Vanish
EDGES Book 9-Chase or Die

Bjorn Series Alternate Reading Plan

1st	Edges Book 1
2nd	Edges Book 2
3rd	Gone Book 1
4th	Firebrand Vol 1
5th	Edges Book 3
6th	Firebrand Vol 2
7th	Gone Book 2
8th	Gone Book 3
9th	Firebrand Vol 3
10th	Gone Book 4
11th	Firebrand Vol 4
12th	Gone Book 5
13th	Gone Book 6
14th	Edges Book 4
15th	Firebrand Vol 5
16th	Gone Book 7
17th	Firebrand Vol 6
18th	Gone Book 8
19th	Firebrand Vol 7
20th	Gone Book 9
21st	Firebrand Vol 8
22nd	Gone Book 10
23rd	Firebrand Vol 9
24rd	Gone Book 11
25th	Firebrand Vol 10
26th	Gone Book 12
27th	Gone Book 13
28th	Firebrand Vol 11
29th	Gone Book 14
30th	Firebrand Vol 12
31st	Gone Book 15
32nd	Firebrand Vol 13
33rd	Gone Book 16
34th	Firebrand Vol 14
35th	Gone Book 17
36th	Firebrand Vol15 (End)
37th	Gone Book 18 (End)
38th	Edges Book 5
39th	Edges Book 6
40th	Edges Book 7
41st	Edges Book 8
42nd	Edges Book 9(End)

ACKNOWLEDGMENTS

We acknowledge those who actively build peace. We acknowledge all the selfless talent which contributed to creating meaningful tokens of consideration and sharing. We acknowledge that every person has a daily choice of right or wrong... and we thank you for choosing the right, good, honorable path filled with integrity because that is the difficult and brave path. Small choices today become lasting monuments of loving hope tomorrow.

CONTENTS

0 PREFACE

Previously, we saw that Tweedbottom revealed his true nature while on a walk with Jane. Meanwhile, Button, determined to survive, has decided to boldly hold fast to his beliefs. It was discovered that Uncle Floyd had a journal and we were witness to a secret barn meeting which was how the resistance met, planned, and decided what sacrifices were worth the preservation of freedom.

.

1 CHAPTER 61: (JUNE 1776) The Magistrate's Brother Explains

Four men stood in the foyer of the Hargreaves' residence. Witherspoon remained silently by the front door. Bryce Aiden Tyler awaited a reply from the magistrate's brother regarding why paying off the debt to handle Floyd Hargreaves' body would help him personally.

Magistrate Pinkney interjected, "Oh, forgive my brother, Mr. Tyler... You see,"

Karl Pinkney forced an embarrassed laugh, struggling to find words to explain, "... you see, you may not realize that my brother, here, was found guilty by the Crown for some such something or other and has had all his lands confiscated by the King. I myself had to sell these properties and send the money to England to ensure my brother remained a free man."

"I see. Free but poor," Bryce Aiden replied, "So the money you collect from your various duties, you give to your brother to replenish what the crown took from him for this something or other crime? May I conclude that you never found out what the crime was? That being the brother of a magistrate gave him no advantage whatsoever?"

"Succinct, Mr. Tyler. That is the sum of it," Magistrate Karl Pinkney replied, "Well, I thank you for paying Miss Hargreaves's debt. My brother and I shall be off."

"One moment, Magistrate Pinkney," Bryce Aiden Tyler said stopping the magistrate from leaving, "Then that means the money you were going to collect from Jane Hargreaves was not mandated by the Crown, but by you... and that you are trying to find ways to give money to your brother?"

Defensive, now, Magistrate Karl Pinkney shifted his weight from foot to foot and said, "I am the law, sir. The rules I set are fair and just. My goal is to find truth and justice for the residents I watch over no matter the cost. Any fees I impose are for a just cause, I assure you. I resent any implication of corruption."

"I did not mean to imply, Magistrate Pinkney," Bryce Aiden started, "any inference that you are being unjust at all. I am merely curious as to why your brother has been made destitute for an unclear crime. Sentence appears to have been passed without any trial. This ruling has come from an official across the ocean, who never clarified to you what the crime was and only demanded money. Why would judgment come from across the ocean? Was there a trial?"

The magistrate's brother replied, "There was no trial. Karl, here, is still trying to find out what crime I've been accused of. It was not listed on the orders."

The Magistrate's brother looked at the writing desk in the foyer but a few feet away as he continued, "What was listed was the mandate to sell all my goods and send the money into the king's coffers. Karl was also told that if he didn't sell off my goods, Karl would be thrown in prison himself."

The Magistrate's brother snapped the official canceled debt papers from the hands of Bryce Aiden Tyler and walked boldly to the writing desk. He took the quill, dipping it into the inkwell as he continued, "So to keep us both free, we had to sell everything I had... Slowly, I'm trying to replenish my purse, Mr. Tyler. I am doing this by acting fairly and in accordance with a moral code, which takes a great deal of patience and time."

The Magistrate's brother then scrawling "PAID" on the document, wrote the date on the official paper requesting payment for processing the body of Floyd Hargreaves.

He signed it. He then handed the quill to his brother the magistrate, who reluctantly scribbled his own signature onto the official form, then handed the now-canceled debt paper back to Bryce Aiden Tyler.

Magistrate Karl Pinkney stated with a flourish and bow, "Your receipt and proof of payment for the handling of Floyd Hargreaves' body, Mr. Tyler. The debt owed by Jane Hargreaves has been satisfied in full, sir."

"Thank you, Mr. Pinkney, "Bryce Aiden started, "... and you Magistrate Karl Pinkney. Thank you both for the receipt. But may I say, if the magistrate's own brother can get punished for a crime he knows nothing about... and it is still your job, Magistrate Pinkney, to seek out justice for the residents of these colonies... then..."

"You are not going to get the money back, Mr. Tyler. No, you shall not," Magistrate Karl Pinkney scoffed.

"Oh, I would not ask for the return of money I have just now given you to to pay Jane Hargreaves's debt, Magistrate Pinkney," Bryce Aiden explained. "But I would ask that you consider the matter of the death of Floyd Hargreaves."

"In what respect should I consider the death?   The   matter   is   closed. Self-murder!" Magistrate Karl Pinkney retorted.

"Witherspoon   and   I   have   been examining the facts, once more," Bryce Aiden explained. "Miss Hargreaves, Mr. Floyd Hargreaves's distraught niece, has gone on her own investigation to discover the truth. Given that: I have paid Jane Hargreaves's debt promptly; given that this money is to help replenish the money the Crown has taken from your brother; given that you and your brother are understandably frustrated about the vague charges against him and a seemingly capricious judgment, which demanded his entire fortune to be sent to the King's coffers in England; given that you just proclaimed your job is to pursue justice and that your authority reaches across vast areas; may I enroll your assistance in finding out the truth as it pertains to Floyd Hargreaves's death? This would give solace to a grieving niece, one of the residents of the colonies you just claimed you defend."

Bryce Aiden paused.

He then added as he reached into his coin purse and extracted another coin, "And this would aid your brother in any expenses he incurs as he watches your post here, while you, Magistrate Pinkney, come with me to find Jane."

Bryce Aiden stopped talking and handed the coin to the Magistrate's brother. The brothers looked at each other for a long silent moment and then both turned to Witherspoon, who stood upright near the door ready to open it, again. Then, the magistrate looked at Bryce Aiden Tyler, as if trying to assess if he should accept this proposition or not.

"Where has Miss Hargreaves gone?" the Magistrate asked Witherspoon.

"She found an invitation sent to her Uncle Floyd. She has decided to attend the event her uncle was invited to and has taken her maid, Silversmith, to the estate of a Lady Sarah Wilson to see an operatic performance by an Irish opera singer, Henry Mossop."

"So, she is not in town, here?" The Magistrate's brother asked. "She's gone for a little holiday?"

Bryce Aiden explained as he tugged down on the hem of his waistcoat as if he were presenting in front of a large crowd, "Miss Hargreaves's uncle was invited to an operatic event, but my deceased business partner hated the opera. Absolutely despised it. So, Miss Hargreaves took it upon herself to find out why he was invited and has taken his place. I believe your investigative skills, Magistrate Pinkney, would be most helpful to resolve any open questions Miss Hargreaves may have about her Uncle's death, and she can tranquilly return home. However, if it was murder and she has taken her uncle's place, then the same people who killed Floyd Hargreaves may also try to harm Jane Hargreaves... In the meantime, your duties here would be covered by your brother..."

"Are you saying you suspect," Magistrate Pinkney stated, "that Floyd Hargreaves's death was not self- murder? I have heard gossips in town sharing their ideas... some from Indian spirits and ghosts said to have taking his life, onward to various conspiracies involving corrupt men of business."

"Yes," Bryce Aiden concurred, "I have heard the same stories, but if Floyd Hargreaves was uncovering a scheme to blame the Indians..."

"Mr. Tyler," the Magistrate interrupted, "I am not interested in town gossip."

Bryce refused to be silenced and continued, "...schemes to blame the Indians for various crimes so the people fear the Indians instead of the people hiring them, who might even be their own neighbors... these are not stories, but notions my deceased business partner, Floyd Hargreaves, had told me on several occasions. I dismissed them at the time as you are now doing. But perhaps there is validity or a grain of truth in these notions he had that the Indians were being hired to commit kidnappings and other crimes."

"Crimes? You mean abducting people to become slaves? Those native tribes have been raiding from one another for centuries!" the Magistrate scoffed. "And slavery has been legal in all thirteen colonies for about a score and five or six years, since 1750, if memory serves me correctly."

"Yes, yes," Bryce waved his hands as if

he knew all that, but was trying to get the magistrate to consider another perspective. He continued, "But the men who hire these Indians are the same ones who purposely kept alliances unbalanced with the natives by making large land deals and then tricking the tribes and breaking those agreements."

"Mr. Tyler," the magistrate snapped, "There is conflict all around us. Last year, in 1775 there were too many battles to mention. This year, the new year, started out with the burning of Norfolk, Virginia. The next month, the colony of North Carolina endured the Battle of Moore's Creek Bridge. The following month of March was the Battle of the Rice Boats in the colony of Georgia, then the Bahamas were raided in Nassau to resupply the Patriots, who later had a victory in Massachusetts by ending that month long conflict at Bunker Hill in Boston. A week later in Quebec, Canada, the Patriots won again at the *Battle of Sain-Pierre.* Then in April, Rhode Island had a battle. In May, the British retaliated and won at the Battle of the

Cedars in Quebec and just this month of June, on the 8th, the British won the *Battle of Trois Rivieres*, forcing the Patriots to evacuate Quebec." He took a breath, "Need I remind you, Mr. Tyler, that I am paid by the British Crown to keep the peace while this revolution against the King of England rages around us..."

"I see," Mr. Pinkney turned to the Magistrate, his brother, and shared, "that the Patriots from the Colonies are protesting against the Loyalists of England. However, despite that, I... as your brother... as brother to a loyal magistrate of the Crown... have not been made immune to the abuses of the Crown and that does make me somewhat sympathetic to the Patriots."

"Enough!" The Magistrate snapped back at his brother, "We mustn't share our personal ordeals with the residents of any of the Colonies. We don't know who knows whom and we must always present loyalty to the King when in public."

The Magistrate's brother retorted to the Magistrate, "The Patriots are simply frustrated at a capricious and greedy Crown for the same injustices as have happened to me. To both you and me, Karl. Just because you are paid by the Crown does not make you immune to its abuses. Perhaps, Karl, you should listen to the plea of this citizen, Mr. Tyler, and ease the grieving niece by finding out the truth of her Uncle's death. I can mind your post here. It should not take you long."

Magistrate Karl Pinkney took a deep breath and moved his gaze from his brother to Bryce Aiden Tyler. "Floyd Hargreaves died a couple months ago. Jane Hargreaves left to stay at some estate... so what of it!"

"She is visiting the estate of Lady Sarah Wilson to attend an Opera sung by Henry Mossop," the butler Witherspoon interjected, then cleared his throat.

The magistrate continued to direct his

attention at Bryce, "Your Miss Jane Hargreaves has been gone for quite some time. If there is another conflict between the Patriots and the British, I am expected to somehow address it... and I do not know which side will earn my brother's sympathies. If he chooses the side of the Patriots, that may injure my income with the crown or get me killed! Why should any of this Indian nonsense matter to me? What has this to do with the death of Floyd Hargreaves?" the magistrate demanded.

Bryce took a deep breath and spoke carefully, "Magistrate Pinkney. I appreciate that these are not peaceful times. I must, however, urge you to please devote some of your investigative talents to this matter of Floyd Hargreaves' death."

Magistrate Pinkney sighed and asked, "What is your theory about the events surrounding Mr. Hargreaves' demise?"

2 CHAPTER 62: (JUNE 1776) Billy and Silversmith Riding To Meeting Town

The horse's coats glistened with sweat as they raced along the road in the blazing heat of the late June sun. Billy Dawes snapped the reins to keep the horses galloping toward Meeting Town.

Next to him on the perch of the carriage, sat Silversmith, clinging with white knuckles to the edge of her seat. She felt every bump in the road and had to keep her lips closed so dust and bugs would not fly into her mouth. Her eyes squinted. Tears rolled from the outer corners of her eyes as the wind whipped her face. She was glad she had tied a ribbon around her simple straw woven hat into a bow under her chin so that it would not fly off.

"How quickly did your mistress say she wanted to find out?" Billy Dawes shouted at Silversmith over the noise of wooden carriage wheels and galloping hooves thudding along the dirt road.

Silversmith shouted a reply, "Miss Jane said she overheard Elizabeth Timothy or Susanna Wright were names of women who could introduce her to Benjamin Franklin. She didn't know which woman we'd find, so she said one or the other is sufficient. She knows I may not be able to locate either, but I'm to send her letters of progress."

"Why does she need to meet Mr. Franklin?" Billy drawled back, with a bit of saliva slipping out of the corner of his mouth from the air current blowing into his face.

"Miss Jane," Silversmith started while they hit another bump and she put one hand on her head to make sure her hat was still secure, "wants to honor her Uncle and Polly Mulhoolin, by asking Mr. Franklin to write a letter to the king to stop the slave trade here."

"Even the Bible," Silversmith started, "Says to stop slavery."

"Indeed?" Billy asked.

"Yes," Silversmith replied, "Jeremiah 34:17 says something like the Lord says that because you have not obeyed God by releasing your country men free to liberty, God will release you to be freely destroyed by war, disease, and famine. You will be an object of horror to all the nations of the earth. I should get to my Bible to get it exactly right."

Billy replied, "It sounds like God was upset with whoever he was talking to. As if he was saying if that because he disobeyed God and he enslaved people, then he would himself become enslaved by war and disease and other terrible things." Billy shrugged and yelled, "But, too many people make too much money to have slavery stopped."

"Well, then they must stop enslaving colonist residents!" Silversmith shouted back. "If we don't stop the slavery of colonists, other sorts of people and nationalities will become victims of slavery."

"You can't save everybody," Billy warned. "Even the fellow who discovered this land, Christopher Columbus, probably had slaves. Probably treated 'em terrible. But, because he could make money for his monarchy, he kept on mistreating people."

"Oh Billy," Silversmith shouted in reply, "Let us simply focus on our task."

"Task?" Billy replied simply.

Silversmith cleared her throat and held up a hand to enumerate all the points they needed to address, "Miss Jane needs an introduction to Mr. Franklin. Miss Jane must be introduced by either Elizabeth Timothy or Susanna Wright as those are the only two women we know of who could foster an introduction."

Billy nodded, indicating he understood.

Silversmith held up a second finger to emphasize her next train of logic. "Because those two converse secretly somewhere in Meeting Town, it is up to us to locate Mrs Timothy or Miss Wright, find out the date of the next *rendezvous*, get one of those women to agree to meet Miss Jane and then to also introduce her to Mr. Franklin."

Billy nodded silently, again.

Satisfied Billy was in agreement, Silversmith lowered her hand to finalize the last portion of the plan, "After that is all arranged, then you may return to Lady Sarah Wilson's estate."

"But if we discover a future date of this secret meeting?" Billy queried.

Silversmith reminded, "You must inform her that you will transport Miss Jane back to Meeting Town to be introduced to Mr. Franklin at the appropriate time."

"I see," Billy yelled hoarsely in reply, then spit out a bug which had just flown into his mouth. There was a long silence.

"They say," Silversmith started, "Mr. Franklin represents Pennsylvania, Georgia, New Jersey and Massachusetts…"

"Hmm," Billy Dawes replied, trying to keep his mouth shut.

"Didn't Polly Mulhoolin mention that when her husband first arrived here, that he worked in a colony called Georgia?" Silversmith asked, then spat out some dust which had billowed up after the carriage wheel hit a dirt clod in the road.

"I do not recall if 'Georgia' is a physical location or the name of the group of people who settled there or something else, but he is *'from Georgia'*, I believe is how the phrase was stated. It is a southern location."

Billy Dawes shrugged. Silversmith remembered she spoke with Polly much more than Billy did. Billy looked at Silversmith. They had a ways to go, yet.

Billy commented, "I think Benjamin Franklin is in Philadelphia, part of some continental congress. I don't think he'd be here, but... if your Miss Jane wants us to search... then..." His voice trailed off.

Silversmith shared, "Perhaps Miss Jane doesn't need to meet with Mr. Franklin, after all... but she may need to convince him to do something so that attacks on Colonists, like the one suffered by Polly Mulhoolin and her husband, never happens again. Miss Jane needs to do something to honor her Uncle Floyd before she can return home and resume a normal life..."

Silversmith then suggested, "We could be done with this in a couple of days, I think."

"What was her uncle working on, then?" Billy Dawes asked as he slowed the horses to a stop. It was time to give them a rest.

As he halted the horses on the road and climbed down from his perch atop the carriage, he went around to help Silversmith down. Billy grabbed the bridal of the lead horse and walked forward, guiding the animals to cool them down.

Silversmith, walking along side Billy, unfolded a letter and looked closely at Billy Dawes as she spoke, "Jane's Uncle Floyd's butler, Witherspoon, the one who brought you in to be hired by Miss Jane, has been writing to me."

"Yes?" Billy drawled.

Silversmith continued, "Mr. Bryce Aiden Tyler was Floyd Hargreaves's business partner. Well, both Mr. Tyler and Witherspoon have been examining the room where Mr. Hargreaves died. They found a notebook or journal of some sort. In there is says Mr. Hargreaves had been meeting with an English speaking native, but Witherspoon didn't write his name in this letter."

"There are several tribes who have learned English, or French... Could be anybody." Billy Dawes commented.

Silversmith read a line in the letter, then looked up, "It seems this particular man was tall. He had asked Mr. Hargreaves for help. He felt the tribes were being blamed for kidnapping and enslaving of colonists, when only a few had agreed to be paid for that service."

"Who by?" Billy asked.

"Witherspoon says they were being paid by British and Irish men of business. He wanted to find out more, then approach Benjamin Franklin to ask him to make some sort of law of the land to stop the practice."

"I don't think anybody would like being removed from the comforts of home and forced into slavery against their will... but..." Billy noted, "we can't stop it. It's a profitable business..."

Silversmith added, "Anyway, that's why she wants to find Mr. Franklin. Miss Jane wants to finish what her Uncle started. Then, Miss Jane can worry about where she will live and how much staff she can afford to maintain."

"I've seen the finery your Miss Jane dresses in. I don't think you'll be lacking for comforts," Billy smirked.

"Oh, those are older fashions we brought from Europe," Silversmith explained. "Miss Jane is on an allowance now which only provides for her and salary for me. I don't think we can afford the maintenance of Mr. Hargreaves' household. I do not think she can afford to pay Witherspoon or any butler's salary, let alone the cost to simply maintain the house if it were empty. And I don't know, Billy, if Miss Jane can afford to keep you on after this mission is complete."

"You'd never know her troubles to speak with her..." Billy commented.

"Oh, she is not one to whine and complain about her circumstances, Mr. Billy Dawes." Silversmith scoffed, "She's well bred, you see. Always concerned for the betterment of others..."

"Call me Billy, please." Billy Dawes smiled, "We best be continuing on, now... best to get there before sunset. Do you want to sit inside or ride up with me?"

"With you," blushed Silversmith smiling.

Billy offered a hand to help her back up to her perch atop the carriage.

Then, he walked around, petting the horses as he moved with a new spring in his step. He bounded up to the perch and with a grin, snapped the reins and they were on their way.

Silversmith added, "Miss Jane gave me enough money to buy two rooms at the inn. One for me and one for you."

"I appreciate that," Billy commented. "It'll be nice to not sleep in the stables."

"Two rooms," Silversmith clarified blushing, "not one..." Silversmith cleared her throat and looked off to one side, watching the scenery whip by.

"Two rooms, two nights, and then hunt down two ladies." Billy smiled to himself, "Mrs. Elizabeth Timothy or Susanna Wright..." Billy looked at Silversmith. She glanced at him as he smiled at her, and then blinked, looking down at her own folded hands.

Billy said, "You think we can find either of these two ladies for your Miss Jane?"

3 CHAPTER 63: (JUNE 1776) The Magistrate Listens to Bryce's Theory

Still standing inside the Hargreaves' foyer, but feet away from the study where Floyd Hargreaves had been found dead, magistrate Karl Pinkney finally agreed to granting a few moments of his time to listen to Bryce Aiden Tyler's theory about events surrounding the death of his business partner.

Karl Pinkney's brother, the magistrate Karl Pinkney himself, Witherspoon the butler, and Bryce Aiden Tyler all stood near the front door.

Bryce began his reply to the magistrate's query for information. He started to explain his hypothesis regarding Floyd Hargreaves' murder, and how it could very well be one element in a larger scheme.

Bryce added, "Imagine a calculated effort of these... I shall call them men of business, for I know not how else to refer to them... These men of business keep encouraging the Indian tribes to resent all colonial residents claiming it is new colonials who cause the land agreements to be broken. Then, these men of business turn to the colonial residents and sow fear among them by hiring some tribes to mar colonist property and person. So, it is these very same men of business who fuel the hatred on all sides."

The Magistrate motioned, "Go on, Mr. Tyler."

Bryce inhaled and continued, "Do you, in fact, understand my hypothesis? Unknowingly, the colonial residents learn to fear the tribes and the tribes resent the residents all because of a calculated manipulation executed by corrupt business men who encourage this feud in order to hide their profitable dealings! Both parties are too busy hating each other to worry about any crimes being conducted against them by these same men of business."

"That is quite a lengthy sentence, Mr. Tyler. What are you really saying?" the magistrate prodded.

Bryce replied with, "There are no laws of this land which prevent these men of business from profiting by these immoral, although legal, activities."

"Now wait, sir. This land is just forming and each colony has its own ways and standards..." the magistrate defended.

"But because something is technically

legal," Bryce Aiden started, "does not mean it is moral or even right. We all know stealing is wrong, but how is it punished? If faceless men of business can steal with an elaborate ruse, why are they not punished as severely as the starving waif who steals a loaf of bread from the market? Why is there this inconsistency of consequences for wrong doings? The business man steals far more, yet does not seem to get any punishment. Yet the waif who steals out of need is imprisoned. If that waif is a slave, then he can be killed with no consequence."

The magistrate clenched his jaw, "I only uphold the law. I do not create it. I do not pass moral judgment on what is right or wrong."

Bryce tried to explain, "We cannot identify these men of business, but they continue to hide behind a curtain of fear and chaos to get away with an even more lucrative crime." Bryce turned to the magistrate's brother, "Do you see?"

The magistrate's brother replied, "Karl, I think I see what Mr. Tyler is trying to explain. There is a cycle. The men of business sell ammunition to the Indians. The Indians attack the colonists and destroy their property with that ammunition. The same men of business sell both repair supplies and more ammunition to the colonists. They encourage the colonial residents to defend their families and property and to keep rebuilding. These men of business then accuse the Indians of destruction while all along the men of business are the ones which encourage it so they can maintain their sales."

"You mean," the magistrate now realized, "That the same men of business are selling ammunitions to both sides and encouraging them to attack each other?"

"Yes," the magistrate's brother affirmed, now understanding, "They would never profit if relations were peaceful. To remain in business they must encourage a feud between at least two parties."

The magistrate turned to Bryce Aiden Tyler and asked, "Are you saying that these men of business promote skirmishes, under the guise of protecting one's family, a noble cause for any man to take up? I want to be quite clear. Are you saying it is the same merchants who promise to provide tools of protection to the very same customer they are secretly trying to destroy and encourage fear in order to sell that customer more goods?"

"Precisely," Bryce Aiden smiled, "And this is why I believe Floyd Hargreaves was murdered. He discovered proof. You see, he told me his theory and I did not pay it much mind, but now if he has been murdered, it must be quite true."

The magistrate's brother spoke up, "So are these skirmishes between the Indians and the colonists... they only occur because everybody's attentions are diverted to focus on this new revolt against our King, yes? If we were at peace, those men of business would not be able to profit by creating further conflict, which has nothing to do with the great revolution for freedom in which we find ourselves?"

Magistrate Pinkney stood silent for a moment. Then said, "But this is merely your hypothesis, Mr. Tyler. You have no proof of the motives of these mysterious faceless men of business."

Bryce Aiden started to reply but Magistrate Pinkney continued, "These are just tales from a dead Floyd Hargreaves." Magistrate Pinkney paused and took a breath, crossing his arms, "Do you, however, Mr. Tyler, have an explanation about how another person could have murdered Floyd Hargreaves when his body was found in a room locked from the inside?"

Bryce started to reply, but was interrupted again by the Magistrate, "I wish to clarify and ask... can you convince me, with objective facts... not your personal opinion... that this was murder and not self-murder?"

Bryce Aiden now smiled. He paused to

see if the magistrate would say something else and then Bryce Aiden Tyler replied. He was now satisfied that the magistrate might actually be willing to help, "We have some more analysis to do, but let me show you what Witherspoon and I have discovered so far. Objective evidence and facts, sir."

The Magistrate's brother suggested, "I can finish collecting from the others on my own, Karl. After that, I can do your rounds and send some of your things over here if you plan to travel. I'll be fine until you return."

"Have you a wife to notify?" Bryce Aiden asked.

Turning red, Magistrate Pinkney replied, "I am a widower, sir. I live with my brother, now. I will hear what you and Witherspoon have to say. I trust my brother to mind things."

"Splendid," Bryce Aiden clapped his hands together, "Then you shall not be constrained by a return date."

The magistrate's brother replied, "Should not take you very long at all, Karl. I'll be able to manage around here until you finish with your inquiries. I mean I don't have enough money to go anywhere else, now do I? Crown's taken it all, haven't they?" He laughed to himself and then smiled at the Hargreaves butler and said, "Witherspoon? Good day to you. To you all."

Witherspoon opened the door, but only the Magistrate's brother left.

Witherspoon closed the door behind him and turned to Magistrate Karl Pinkney and said, "Would you like a cup of tea, sir? To explain may take a while."

"Yes, I would, thank you, Witherspoon," the magistrate replied.

After Magistrate Karl Pinkney's brother left the Hargreaves residence, the Magistrate accepted Witherspoon's offer for tea.

Bryce Aiden Tyler, business partner to the deceased Floyd Hargreaves, whose body was discovered in the study, had convinced the magistrate to listen to a theory, which might help prove Floyd Hargreaves was murdered.

On his way to the kitchen, Witherspoon whispered in Bryce's ear, "Sir, if what you said earlier is plausible and Miss Jane took her uncle's place, and her uncle was murdered, would not Miss Jane be in danger?"

Bryce whispered back, "Yes. Exactly. We must move forward, Witherspoon. Go hire a carriage. I'm sure Magistrate Pinkney will want to head over to Lady Sarah Wilson's once he sees what we've discovered."

The curious magistrate asked bluntly, "What are you two discussing there?"

Bryce wanted to get to the facts and present the magistrate with a plausible explanation, which would open an investigation to catch a murderer. He did not want the magistrate to think that he was only putting on a show because Bryce might be overly concerned for Jane's wellbeing. True, he was, but he needed the magistrate's men to agree to help him first.

Bryce replied to the magistrate's inquiry with, "Oh, yes. Serve bread and jam with the tea, Witherspoon," Bryce Aiden added. Then he led Magistrate Karl Pinkney into the study where Floyd Hargreaves died.

"While we wait for Witherspoon to return with tea," the magistrate cleared his throat, "I would like to have a very clear discussion with you."

"Yes?" Bryce said, "Witherspoon is a capital butler and I believe we have worked it out to disprove the original conclusion. We've been communicating with Jane. Oh, I mean Miss Hargreaves and comparing notes on our investigation. In other words, we can show you how the murderer could have killed Floyd Hargreaves."

"I see. And Miss Jane Hargreaves, the niece, is away? And has been for some time?" the magistrate clarified.

"Yes, but..." Bryce started to say.

"I find this all too convenient, Mr. Tyler," the magistrate explained. "Jane is gone and unavailable to speak with. You are here, and have been able to work out how a murder was committed, and ask for my time... which is time away from my normal duties... to take up an investigation."

"Yes, but let me show you..." Bryce started again.

"I think," the magistrate went on as if Bryce had not said anything at all, "That you are only able to show that it was murder if you, sir, are the one who murdered Floyd Hargreaves."

"I beg your pardon, Magistrate Pinkney!" Bryce stated, his head cocked to one side as if he had not heard the magistrate properly.

"For instance," the magistrate began, "How is it your Jane Hargreaves is unavailable for communication, yet you and that butler Witherspoon seem to be able to keep each other appraised of this so called investigation?"

"Well," Bryce explained, "Witherspoon has a friend on staff in a nearby household. When they head in the direction of Lady Sarah Wilson's estate, Witherspoon scribes a letter to Silversmith, Jane Hargreaves lady's maid, and they drop off the note at the general store in town... or, if they are able, at the estate."

"Earlier," the magistrate responded, "you suggested that I should be occupied with your investigation and not be tied to any return date. Did you not?"

"I did," Bryce replied, "because I did not know how long it would take to locate Jane Hargreaves and make official inquiries. I realize I am an amateur at all this and you are an expert and I would very much like your assistance in discovering the truth."

"Or," the magistrate responded, "did you wish to do away with me, as well?" Magistrate Pinkney looked around at the desk, the window, the burnt bowl, a folded paper box, and the child's toy magnetic fishing pole all laying out on the table in an orderly manner as if ready for a demonstration.

Witherspoon entered the study with a tray of tea for the two gentlemen and set it down on a table.

"What are you saying, Magistrate Pinkney?" Bryce asked as he glanced at Witherspoon indicating that he should stay.

"I am saying quite plainly," the magistrate calmly stated with twisted smile on one side of his mouth, "that you can only show me how a self-murder was actually a murder if you yourself were the one committing the crime."

Witherspoon realizing the gravity of the

conversation raised both eyebrows quite against his will.

"Are you, Magistrate Pinkney," Bryce spoke very deliberately, "accusing me of killing my own business partner and... and..."

The magistrate picked up a cup of tea, sat down and took a sip of the brew. He looked up at Bryce and helped him finish his sentence.

"and...," the magistrate started, "confessing to me how you did it with those things you have displayed there... and as civilized gentlemen over tea. Yes. Yes, I am." And he took another sip.

Witherspoon cleared his throat.

"Yes!" Bryce Aiden Tyler snapped at the butler.

"Sir, shall I summon the boy I sent to fetch a driver and cancel the carriage to Lady Sarah Wilson's estate?"

Abruptly, Magistrate Karl Pinkney put down his teacup and blurted out, "What is that? Some sort of secret panel?"

Magistrate Karl Pinkney's keen eye for detail had noticed something which both Witherspoon and Bryce Aiden Tyler had not seen before.

4 CHAPTER 64: (JUNE 1776) Secret Barn Meeting-Button Daydreams

Button was growing weary of serving water at these various secret meetings.

Farmer and Tallman had promised Button would meet somebody to shed light on the whereabouts of his missing wife, but alas he encountered no person who could tell him anything of value.

This particular barn smelled like horsehair, freshly smelted blacksmith's horseshoes, hay and manure.

One man, without looking at Button, held his goblet up expecting it to be filled with water. Only then, did Button awaken out of his day dream and fill the goblet with water.

Only then, did Button start listening to what was being said. Slowly, a soup of feelings started welling up inside him. He didn't know why, but he felt suspicious, doubtful, frustrated and impatient.

Was he feeling guilty about the raid on his own home? Could he have done anything more to protect his wife and their unborn child? Their home? Button shook his head. No. He had done all that one man could have done.

Button was jarred from his thoughts by a comment from the speaker.

"...have we indefinite indifference on this matter?" The speaker asked the crowd, "...is this not why we meet in clandestine chambers? Then, should we not do something about it?"

Button wondered what the man was saying. Perhaps he should stop dwelling on his own problems and listen.

The speaker pointed to another man and accused, "This fellow, known for his penmanship, succumbs to fret and fears. He is unable to write what we need him to pen because you all share his fears of certain defeat." The speaker took a drink. Draining his goblet and placing it down, he continued, "Once we band together on this, we will strengthen him, the letter shall be penned, and our task is done as if we were all of one mind. What say you?" And the speaker sat down.

Button weaved through the crowd with his jug and filled the goblet of the speaker, who smiled and nodded a thanks to Button.

A woman stood up to comment.

It was not customary for women to speak, but in these secret meetings, the rules of tradition were violated in order to more efficiently address the subjects at hand. She addressed the attendees, "We need him to write down what we will and will not accept from the Crown. I endorse the notion that all colonies should be united unanimously in support of Mr. Livingston's effort."

A third person stood and said, "We must obtain redress of our grievances, which threaten destruction to our lives, our liberty, and the property of all his majesty's subjects in North America."

"My good sirs," The original speaker retorted, "Our thoughts are still jumbled. How do you want him to write down our thoughts on a non-importation, non-consumption and non-exportation agreement?" The man stopped short as if to gather his thoughts.

"I think what you are trying to say..." The man Farmer pointed out to be Benjamin Franklin earlier now stood up to share his thoughts.

Mr. Franklin said, "...Is should all the colonies agree... Should we unite under the ties of virtue, honor, and love of this new country, then I can carry a letter to the King and explain that this option you suggest will be the most speedy and peaceable path, free of bloodshed..."

"As an example, Mr. Franklin." Another stood to comment, "If I can summarize of what we speak in an example... If the colonies agreed to not import, say tea from East India into British America from Great Britain, nor Ireland, nor Dominica, nor Madeira, nor any of the crown's other colonies..."

"Then," Mr. Franklin interrupted, "You would also need to add to that list... avoid the import of not only East India tea, but molasses, syrup, panels, coffee, pimento from the Dominica plantations, wines from Madeira or any of the Western Islands, including indigo dyes."

A woman smiled, "Mr. Franklin, I am working on increasing the growth of Indigo with another woman who is meeting me here in this town. Together we shall strategize to manufacture blue dyes here and even create sufficient amounts to export it. I am able to provide you with sample dyed silks which rival those of the Far East. You may take them on your next voyage to England to Queen Charlotte to demonstrate our capabilities."

"Thank you, Miss Wright," Mr. Franklin smiled. Then to the crowd, "May you all follow the spirit of Susanna Wright, here, who is actively building solutions for this new country's economy." Mr. Franklin continued, "We shall become self-sufficient here in British America. And now, it is imperative that I broach a delicate subject upon which I know this room is divided." Franklin took a deep breath, looked sternly about the room, and said, "I believe we must neither import... nor purchase... any more slaves."

Button felt a shock of lightning up his spine. He was very alert, now. Was it the intention of this meeting to address a subject, which impacted Button directly? He picked up his jug of water and filled another's goblet, while keeping his eye on this Benjamin Franklin fellow.

"I agree, Sir," John Hancock stated. "In fact, simply because I am a gentleman and land owner does not stop me from paying for my labor instead of forcing slaves to work."

Button, realizing all these men had such clear opinions, wondered if he had not been a bit cowardly by not taking a side on an issue and not standing up for it. He did, after all, marry a woman who had, firsthand, experience of indentured servitude and be she alive or dead, was that not enough to make Button have a voice on this subject?

Still, Button said nothing and just listened.

Samuel Adams stood up, and all eyes turned to him. "Indeed, you are familiar with the residents of the Maine area: John Hancock Abigail Bromfield, along with a handful of others... all are determined to manage their lands with honor. That means paying fair wages to our workers. I ask each of you to recall why you or your parents left Britain and suffered a harsh voyage to establish a new life here. Was it not because of the way you had been treated? In this new land, we cannot bring destructive traditions with us. We must change how we manage people. We can build a thriving economy without the broken backs of slaves. "

Button looked across the room and noticed Farmer was simply filling goblets with water. Button stayed on his side of the room and wondered If the entire country agreed to abolish slavery, then he would not have been kidnapped... and he would not need to worry about future raids... He could still cling to his dream of starting his own family... assuming Polly was still alive, that is.

"My good man!" Henry Mossop, stood up and protested. Button recalled that Farmer had identified this man earlier as a singer from Ireland.

Henry Mossop continued, "Are you suggesting to wholly discontinue the slave trade? Do you also propose not to hire our own vessels, nor sell our commodities nor our manufactures? If so, you are asking for great sacrifice of comforts." Henry Mossop made it clear he was not pleased with the direction this meeting was taking. Those standing around Henry Mossop murmured in agreement.

Mr. Samuel Adams replied, "Mr. Mossop. You are not even a permanent resident in these lands. You have repeatedly been vocal about how temporary your visit is here."

"That does not matter," Mossop replied challengingly, "And it is 'sir', not 'mister'. I still have a voice and can state my opinion. I might change my mind and stay here... Now, are you too cowardly to address my concerns in this forum?"

Mr. Adams took a deep breath, "Mister Mossop," he started deliberately, "His majesty, King George, has imposed duties on all glass, all painter's colors... including indigo," Samuel Adams glanced at Susanna Wright, the woman who had just proclaimed she planned to develop enough indigo dyes to export.

He returned his gaze to the red-faced Henry Mossop.

Samuel Adams continued, "...paper, teas and he has mandated that they must be imported only from Britain since he passed the Revenue Act a decade ago in 1767. Be it of good quality or poor, we must accept it. Why are we not permitted to import only what WE judge as the best quality? I understand our clamorings have resulted in the Act's partial repeal back in 1770, but this is not enough. Nay. Our only hope is to invent here on our soil, a better product which we do not need to import... and can even make enough of to export in sufficient quantity."

He smiled at Susanna Wright, again. She nodded her acknowledgment in reply.

"Your reasoning for this is because His Majesty still wishes to increase the price of tea?" Mossop retorted scoffing as if Mr. Adam's argument was insufficient to sway anybody.

Mr. Adams continued, now fully turning to Henry Mossop, "If His Majesty's ships succeed in the sale of that tea, we shall have no property that we can call our own. And then we may bid adieu to American liberty."

Mr. Franklin stood up to assist Mr. Adams in his argument. "What Mr. Adams clearly is saying is that to contribute to the support of the common liberties of America, we must all agree to associate together. Faithfully and united under one name. Perhaps something like the Sons of New York."

That comment elicited a cacophony of murmurs from the crowd.

"If I may, gentlemen," Susanna Wright spoke as she stood up, "For those old enough, I would like you to recall the

1730's. There was an abundance of bored widows... The women would host parties and invite each other over to assuage their loneliness."

A belligerent man interrupted her, "We are here to discuss issues, Madam. Sit down."

Susanna Wright looked at Benjamin Franklin, who said to the crowd, "Let her speak. Listen to her insights."

Susanna Wright continued speaking to the group, "I was told that in Virginia, Widow Degraffenreidt and Widow Stagg tried to compete with each other to host the best ball. Widow Stagg lured attendees by offering a young male slave as a raffle prize. Not to be outdone by Widow Stagg, Widow Degraffenreidt raffled a slave woman and her child as a prize at her ball. Certainly this occurred a score of years ago,"

Susanna Wright paused and looked each man in the eye before continuing, "I ask you to consider... is that how you want the reputation of this new land, this 'free' British America, this collection of Sons of Liberty, as Mr. Franklin suggested... is this how you want to be known? A country where, for entertainment, a woman and her child are given away as slave prizes?"

Susanna took a breath and then continued as she changed her tone of voice, "Join me in my pursuits to discover new quality products we can make in this country in sufficient quantities to export. Think about developing something to fortify the purses of this country whatever its name shall be. I am collaborating with a woman, Eliza Lucas, to teach others to cultivate indigo plants. I am developing fine silk fabrics to surpass the quality of those we currently import. We do not need slaves. We do not need to treat humans whose hands are calloused by cruelly unremitting labor... with cavalier disdain. We need quality, skilled, properly paid, and appreciated craftsmen to help us develop the economy of this new and wondrous country."

"You don't understand, Miss Wright. You are a Quaker... and a woman..." One man dismissed without standing up, "you are not capable of understanding business".

"As you may or may not know," Miss Wright calmly replied, "My father was a physician. I would frequently assist him by performing the duties of a physician."

"You were not schooled to be a doctor!" Another protested.

"Correct, Sir." Miss Wright agreed, "Few women have the advantage to be formally schooled, so I learned from my father and was formally educated in England."

"You should 'ave stayed there, Miss," another anonymous voice commented.

Unperturbed, Susanna Wright continued, "Although I could have stayed, I wanted to pursue my freedom of religion and explore the talents with which God gifted me. I could do that here in this country. Not England. In Lancaster, Pennsylvania, I created libraries with volumes in Italian, Latin, French and English. It was here, Gentlemen, that I had the opportunity to experiment with cultivating silkworms, weaving of fabrics, and using Eliza Lucas' indigo plants to dye those silks. In addition to my naturalist and medicinal talents, I have been able to help my community in their legal and property disputes. But, business aside, I have also been able to pursue my love of poetry and paint. My talents as a free British American woman have allowed me to make my local community a better and more profitable place. I wish to emphasize that I would not have these opportunities back in England..."

Susanna Wright stood motionless for a moment, then took a deep breath, and said,

"Therefore, I ask all of you to please listen to Mr. Franklin, Mr. Adams, Mr. Livingston and Mr. Hancock. We must not revert to the ways of the country we left behind. We must document a better way…" and Miss Wright sat down.

The attendees silently glanced at each other uncertain what to say next.

"If we," Mr. Hancock stated as he slowly rose to applaud Miss Wright's comments, "Are to heed Miss Wright's business advice, this new document must be stronger than the Articles of Association written in 1774."

A voice from the crowd protested, "Congress in Philadelphia already tried and failed to prohibit trade with Great Britain."

"But there is strength in numbers. It must be all of us!" Mr. Adams underscored.

Through the slats of the barn, the attendees could hear the bleating of sheep in the distance, and then, a dog barking, presumably to round up the stray sheep for the shepherd.

Another member of the crowd stood up, "On the fifth day of September in 1774, It was all of us, sir!"

He held out his hand as he started to demonstrate by counting his fingers. "Need I remind all of you, it was the colonies of New Hampshire, Massachusetts Bay, Rhode Island, Connecticut, New York, New Jersey, Pennsylvania, the three lower counties of Newcastle, Kent and Sussex on Delaware, Maryland, Virginia, North Carolina, and South Carolina. It failed in '74, there is no point in trying it again two years later."

Henry Mossop added, "What we need to do is acknowledge we are loyal British American subjects. What I mean to say is if we unite in allegiance and affection to the King of England, we will all be well cared for. It is a waste of time to pen any letter to His Majesty asking for independence. It would be better to write of our undying allegiance to the Crown."

Mr. Franklin turned to Henry Mossop protesting, "Listen. His Majesty wishes to enslave our colonies. This causes alarming anxiety and apprehensions due to King George's constant oppression. He has arbitrarily accused those living here of crimes, which the accused do not know they have committed, yet they are either jailed or all their possessions are liquidated and proceeds sent to the king's treasury."

Mr. Adams agreed, "King George has held an illegal constitutional trial beyond the seas without our participation. He has exposed our very lives to grave danger from his arbitrary wars. And, now he has passed an act to extend his provinces to Quebec, Canada?"

Mr. Franklin addressed the crowd, "Are we at an impasse on the matter of slavery? Or on the concept of writing a letter to His Majesty?"

5 CHAPTER 65: (JUNE 1776) Polly learns Mrs. Dunlap's Secret

Polly was sitting on a sofa in the Dunlap printer's study, reading a book. It was just after tea time and Polly's tea cup was drained. The plate before her was just out of reach and she did not have the energy to sit up and lean over her pregnant belly to reach for the last two small tea sandwiches. So Polly continued to read.

Mrs. Dunlap, passing by in the hallway, noticed Polly in the study and walked in.

"On a warm June day, such as this, it is nice to know you are nearing the end of your term, isn't it, Polly dear?" Mrs. Dunlap said as she sat down across from Polly.

Polly put the book down. "I am anxious to be rid of this condition. It has become most uncomfortable," Polly commented and rested the open book on top of her belly, "But I do thank you for housing me all this time. I am quite sure my bacoun payment had run out. I was just noting that it is so gracious of you and your husband to allow me to stay here until my baby arrives. I wish I could do more for your kindness..."

"Oh, Mr. Dunlap," Mrs. Dunlap started, "has been frightfully busy. I've enjoyed your companionship. The days can become tedious without somebody to talk to..." Mrs. Dunlap smiled then brightly added, "But perhaps I should let you know that I have been secretly busy, as well... I mean, during the days you come in here to read, I've been..."

Mrs. Dunlap's voice trailed off and she saw the plate in front of Polly had unfinished tea sandwiches on them. Mrs. Dunlap popped one into her mouth and stopped talking to chew.

"Well, I envy your freedom to go into town, Mrs. Dunlap..." Polly started, "It would be unseemly for me to be seen in public in this condition, yet I do yearn for a stroll amongst people." Polly paused, "But, what have you been..." And Polly looked at Mrs. Dunlap to finish.

"I don't want you to be upset, dear," Mrs. Dunlap shared, then stood up, turning toward the doorway.

"Mrs. Dunlap," Polly started, "Why would I be upset? Do clear things up for me, Mrs. Dunlap." Polly was now getting a bit concerned.

Slowly, Mrs. Dunlap turned back toward Polly, "As you said, you have not left the house... due to your condition..."

"Yes?" Polly prodded.

Mrs. Dunlap paused, "It was an impetuous idea of mine. Foolhardy. I shall reverse what I've done." And she started to stride confidently toward the doorway.

"Mrs. Dunlap," Polly started again, "I'm sure it's not as bad as all that... before you reverse anything, could you kindly enlighten me?"

After a moment of deliberation, Mrs. Dunlap nodded to herself and returned to her seat, sitting down, looking Polly straight in the eye and said, "I've taken a liberty and infringed on your privacy, my dear."

"Indeed?" Polly's eyes widened and she sat up a bit straighter. As straight as she could, given the down filled pillows bolstering her.

"I know," Mrs. Dunlap started, "That the anguish of raising a child on your own is terrifying. The traumatic manner in which you lost your husband... you see, I was simply trying to find a way of comforting you..."

"I'm really not understanding, Mrs. Dunlap. I promise I won't be cross if you simply and bluntly tell me what is afoot," Polly shared with a smile.

Mrs. Dunlap slowly stated, "I wanted to keep my inquires a secret until I was sure. I exhausted all of my connections and my husband's newspaper sources of information. I am sorry to say that I have not heard any news of...."

"Of my husband? Have you been trying to find out what happened to him? If he is alive?" Polly rushed her words.

"That..." Mrs. Dunlap started, "My efforts were a failure. I found out nothing. Nothing about who the raiders were, about... It's just that kidnappings of everyday folk is not news worthy enough, anymore. Especially small gatherings of one to a handful of homes situated in the middle of nowhere..." She paused, "Now if the raid occurred in the center of town, that would be news and my husband

John, I mean Mr. Dunlap said…" She stopped short to see Polly's reaction then continued, "I am so sorry. Your husband might still be alive surviving off the land somewhere. I know it's been some time, but he will search for you… one day…"

"And how will he know I'm here? Only Billy Dawes, Jane Hargreaves, Silversmith and you know I'm here. Even if he were alive, how would he find me…" Polly's voice trailed off, "I suppose I must face the facts and accept that Button is dead…."

Brightly, Mrs. Dunlap added, "But, I felt I needed to tell you that I did investigate… without your permission. And now my conscience is clear."

"Oh, Mrs. Dunlap. Were you concerned I would have felt my privacy invaded? No. I appreciate the effort you made to try and find out more information than I had." Polly forced a smile, disappointed at the results.

"But," Mrs. Dunlap continued, "In the course of my inquiries, I met somebody you would find interesting and perhaps even comforting... shall I ask Simms to fetch more tea for our guests?"

"Guests?" Polly asked, "As in more than one? I'm not in a state to receive any friends, Mrs. Dunlap."

Mrs. Dunlap popped the last tea sandwich into her mouth, stood up still chewing. She strode over to the wall and pulled the woven sash to summon her butler.

"Nonsense," Mrs. Dunlap started, "They are waiting in the parlor for my signal. You'll love them." And then Mrs. Dunlap swallowed the last tea sandwich and smiled brightly.

6 CHAPTER 66: (JUNE 1776) Secret Barn Meeting - Button speaks.

The discussions in this secret barn meeting seemed to simply circle about resulting in no definitive resolution.

This entertaining opera singer from Ireland, Henry Mossop, seemed to be defending the need to use slaves, even though it was primarily his own countrymen, the Irish, who were victims of this practice. He simply disassociated himself from the Irish people, opting rather to attach himself to the British Crown.

Button concluded that he must have done something to develop such a disdain for his own country.

Across the room, Button noticed that the Farmer had been watching Button very carefully. More so than in the past. Button shook his head. He would honor his agreement to help clean up after the meeting ended. He would go home with the Farmer, gather his belongings, and then be off at the break of day.

Through the slats, the late afternoon sun shone shafts into the barn. Sheep dotting the hills of the neighboring farm could be heard bleating in the distance.

Mr. Hancock stood up and addressed the crowd, "If we are not to discuss slavery, let us discuss how we must improve our breed and number of sheep. We must encourage inventors. We must promote agriculture, arts and manufacturing locally in this land. We must encourage thriftiness and frugality."

The hour was slipping away and Button knew the stable boys would soon return and this political meeting would be concluded. Then, he could be on his way to close out this painful chapter and start anew in the morning... somewhere...

To Button's surprise, and for the first time, he saw the Farmer speak in public at these meeting forums.

Farmer said, "I applaud all you educated gents... and lady..." He nodded to Susanna Wright, "But you speak of all this change, yet I have not heard you ask the opinion of a common man."

"Common man?" Mr. Hancock replied, a bit taken aback, and then continued, "We all represent the common people. That is the point of these meetings."

"Then, ask him," Farmer pointed to Button who was filling another goblet and quite flustered at the sudden attention the audience was just now giving to him. "Go on," The Farmer urged, "Ask that man over there about his opinion on colonist slavery and Irish indentureds."

Accepting the challenge, Mr. Hancock turned to Button and said, "What is your name?"

Button looked at Farmer, who was smiling for putting the spotlight onto Button. Button quickly assessed that Farmer must have been prompted to bring attention to Button because he knew Button intended on leaving. From across the room, Farmer smiled at Button, then went to fill a stein being held high in the crowd asking for water. The Farmer succeeded in getting Button involved, much to Button's chagrin.

Annoyed with Farmer, Button took a deep breath to quell his vexation and slowly turned to Mr. Hancock, "My name, Mr. Hancock, is Button, a common man."

"Do common men possess independent thought, Sir? Or do you opt to mirror the views of your master?" Mr. Hancock asked. The room had gone silent and Button was feeling a bit nervous, now.

"Sir?" Button asked, his throat suddenly parched.

"What think you," Mr. Hancock started slowly as if to humor the request of Farmer and be done with it. Mr. Hancock continued with, "...As a common man, tell us how we should handle our affairs in these British Americas as the Sons of New York." Then, distracted he turned to Mr. Franklin and said, "I don't care for that Sons of New York title for the united colonies. We'll have to develop a new name." Then, he casually returned his gaze to Button.

Button stared at a shaft of light penetrating the dark room. The shaft had moved, indicating the sun was nearly ready to set. He heard the sheep outside, punctuated by the occasional oink of a pig and neigh of a horse. He was aware that all eyes were on him, now.

Button took a long breath and said, "Mr. Hancock, Mr. Franklin, Mr. Adams and the rest of you, sirs... I believe..."

"Get on with it!" a man shouted out from the crowd.

Button now had sympathy for when Susanna Wright was speaking earlier, as she had attempted to complete a sentence without these impatient interruptions from the audience.

"I believe," Button started to speed up, "we must sheer our own wool and manufacture our own fabrics. Women should demonstrate frugality when a loved one dies by abandoning the current practice giving of gloves and scarves at funerals. We must discourage the wasteful practice of creating a full mourning dress for that occasion. Instead, let us agree to wear a simple black ribbon on the arm or on the hat for gentlemen; and black ribbon and black necklace for ladies. We must discourage betting on horse races, and cock fighting. We must stop accepting lewd exhibitions as entertainment. We must halt all these habits because when we indulge in them, we support the Crown. The British prey on our vices, and from these vices only the Crown makes a profit at our expense."

After the long silence which followed Button's words, Henry Mossop spoke.

"And what, Mr. Button, do you think of opera singers? Is that considered lewd entertainment?" Henry Mossop stood up as he continued, "I recently performed at the private estate of Lady Sarah Wilson. Was I or my audience lewd or vulgar in that example?" He laughed and those around him laughed as if on cue.

"In England," Button bravely welcomed the stern gaze of this foppishly dressed stout singer, "I had friends who enjoyed luxuries, but in excess. That excess caused corruption. I came to this new country willing to work in the middling trades in the colony of Georgia. I have traveled some, not all, of this land. On the voyage over, I met a learned woman from a similarly privileged background whose fortunes changed due to the capricious flow of political winds of monarchs. She was forced to sign as an indentured servant in exchange for her passage over here. Her integrity and ability to resist vices caused me to fall in love and marry her."

Henry Mossop mockingly clapped, "Well, what a love story. Good performance. You may fetch me some more water, now." He dismissed Button with a gesture.

Henry Mossop was about to address the crowd and was just inhaling to speak when Button replied.

"I was invited to speak by Mr. Hancock, Sir, and I shall complete my thought,"

Button stated walking away from the

water jug and causing Henry Mossop to slowly turn and look at Button.

Button continued, "We married as soon as she fulfilled her contract and became free. We started anew and built our first cabin, able to provide for ourselves, working toward a more noble goal... yet, we were interrupted in our pursuit for liberty and happiness because, Sir, because somebody else thirsted for the profits offered by being a slave trader. My home was raided. I never saw my wife again. I was captured. It was made clear to me I would be sold as a slave. Shortly thereafter I escaped. I was, Sir, intended to be somebody's inventory."

"Escaped? A small band of Indians let you go?" Henry Mossop clarified, now looking at Button very differently. "That is very fortunate indeed..."

"To come to this country cost me dearly. Why must I fight to remain in the home built on land I own? We simply wanted to be left in peace." Button concluded.

Before the opera singer could think of a retort, Button quickly added, "But, I believe it was greed which caused the raid. If the people here can agree to stop the slave trade, then my wife and I could live in peace, build a happy family and even help in providing the skilled labor Miss Wright requires to develop a new industry or product for export. We cannot make this country great, if its residents are never safe to live in their own homes."

"We needn't hear your pitiful story, you never answered my question about lewd entertainment!" Opera Singer Mossop spat.

Button replied with vigor, "If an industry which tears asunder a husband and wife is not enough reason for you, Mr. Mossop, then I would answer you with this: If the price of Opera is costly, making it only an entertainment for the very rich, then to attain admiration, the people may misspend their money to try and attend simply to brag. If it is opera that you crave, we should organize some sort of subsidy to allow all the people access to that or any other art. We must not encourage residents of this land to compete with each other to show they can afford luxuries they perhaps cannot really afford simply to impress their neighbors. We need the people to direct their talents to build this land into a nation."

Mr. Samuel Adams now stood up and addressed Mr. Mossop, "Sir, we asked this man... this common man to speak, yet you attacked him with disrespect. I must conclude that what he said to you injured you in some way. Mr. Mossop, do you profit by being on stage or do you profit by the slave trade?"

Henry Mossop's face turned red, "I did not come here to be insulted, but to warn the people that they would be safer to show allegiance to the King of England."

"The King of England is not normally favored by the Irish," Mr. Adams calmly replied. "And I do not know why you would consider a business question an insult... especially since you just emphasized how normal and everyday slavery should be... as a business..."

"I warn you, sir," Mossop spat.

"Warn me of what, exactly," Mr. Adams demanded then added, "You, sir, Mr. Mossop, have not answered MY question." Mr. Adams reiterated, "Do you profit from the slavery of a captured colonist?"

He turned to Button and pointed, "Would you profit by enslaving this free man, a man some might call... 'Neighbor'?"

"There is nothing illegal in what I do," Mossop protested.

"No, Sir. You are correct," Samuel Adams continued, "...it is legal in all thirteen colonies. In fact, some of us own slaves, but we meet today to determine if being an owner of another human being is moral. And should we encourage men of business to capture random people from their homes in order to support a lucrative yet immoral industry?"

John Hancock now stood up to add to Mr. Adam's point, "This man named Button serves us water, yes, but perhaps he is in possession of another talent. Perhaps we are not allowing him to contribute to the rich tapestry of our New World. Perhaps his energies are spent on trying to escape the men trying to enslave him. Hardly a productive use of either his energy or time."

The red-faced Henry Mossop pointed to every person in the room with angry sputtering words, "Your ridiculous concept of united colonies shall... never... be achieved," Mossop breathed through his nostrils with a spurt akin to a dragon attempting to breathe fire when nothing ignites. "I warn you. You need King George. You are part of the British Empire. Period! You will not survive without his protections in this wilderness!"

81

Mr. Adams calmly commented, "And what if another ambitious merchant thought you, Mr. Mossop, would make a fine candidate for a slave. May we all assume you would be agreeable to that as your new profession?"

Mossop stopped for but a second, broke his gaze from Hancock, and marched over to Samuel Adams with clenched jaw sputtering, "Your insinuation that somebody like me... someone of my station... could be sold as a slave is... preposterous!"

"Is it?" Samuel Adams replied innocently.

With clenched jaw, Henry Mossop stated, "I am entertaining a notion to deprive this entire assembly of my expertise, of my advice. I shall never attend one of these meetings, again!" Henry Mossop seethed. This boastful former opera *primo uomo* breathed heavily enough so that Mr. Adams could smell his breath... and react as politely as a gentleman could to a foul odor.

Henry Mossop mustered up his stage presence to leave. On his way out, Mossop walloped Button with such a blow it caused Button to stagger backwards.

Instinctively, Mossop turned toward his audience to take a bow, expecting to hear applause, but instead he heard gasps of disgust. This was not what Mossop expected.

Two men rushed to Button's side to ensure he was only winded and did not suffer any other physical harm from Mossop's spontaneous attack.

"Sir, what you have done is a grave injustice!" Robert Livingston declared to the flustered former opera singer, Henry Mossop. Livingston continued, "It is a breach of gentlemanly courtesy. I have remained silent during these conversations because, as we mentioned in the beginning, I was unclear about what to write. I was blessed with fine penmanship, yet lacked motivation. This moment has provided me with not only motivation, but clear purpose about what to pen to His Majesty."

"To acquiesce, I trust. To succumb quietly to his rule," Mossop replied.

"No," Robert Livingston corrected, "This meeting has bolstered my confidence that if we unite in this room, we can unite in the colonies. This country will succeed without your brand of capricious justice, Mr. Henry Mossop."

A turbulent conversation ensued about how Henry Mossop had just treated Button. The assembly was now crowding around this very vocal opera singer. One voice shouted, "That's not due process. We need due process in matters such as these…"

Finally, Mossop and his small entourage pushed through the crowd until they got close enough to shove open the barn door.

The crowd then jostled Henry Mossop and the men with him outside, closing the door behind them.

Button was still smarting from the unprovoked blow delivered moments earlier by Mr. Henry Mossop. The crowd's conversation continued to rise in volume.

Punctuating the loud discourse, Robert Livingston stepped up onto a horse stall gate to rise above the crowd and with a booming voice, he declared, "I have witnessed the fortitude of character demonstrated by this common man, Button, who humbly served us sweet water from the Farmer's land."

The crowd cheered in reply.

Mr. Livingston continued, "I am inspired to conclude that every citizen's voice should be heard in a singular united message... A message I will write to his Majesty King George...Have you any objections?" he asked the crowd.

7 CHAPTER 67: (JUNE 1776) Mrs. Timothy Found by Silversmith and Billy! But, wait...

Moving through the streets of Meeting Town, Billy Dawes, carriage driver hired by Miss Jane Hargreaves, was enjoying his time on this mission with Silversmith, Miss Jane's lady's maid. He pointed at a sign, alerting her to a bookstore they were approaching.

Billy asked, "Do you think that shopkeeper inside would know the whereabouts of Elizabeth Timothy or Susanna Wright, the names of the women you overheard could introduce Miss Jane to Benjamin Franklin?"

Silversmith replied, "He may know of Elizabeth Timothy since she's a printer and author. Runs the Southern Carolina Gazette Newspaper, I overheard. Susanna Wright, they said was a Quaker, and has built up a library for her village, but she mostly has been developing silks and dyes. I don't think a man who runs a book shop would know where Susanna Wright could be. Let us ask inside about Elizabeth Timothy. Grand idea of yours, Mr. Billy Dawes. So glad Witherspoon found you and Miss Jane hired you," silversmith grinned

Billy asked, "We only need one woman or the other, right?"

Silversmith replied, "We don't need either if Ben Franklin could convince the Royal Courts of England to halt slave raids on Colonial residents. Then, Miss Jane could both honor the mission of her

Uncle Floyd... may he rest in peace... and help Polly Mulhoolin raise her child in peace, as well."

"I doubt," Billy Dawes said, "Mr. Franklin would accept an invitation from us to meet your Miss Jane..."

"We best go inside that bookshop, then," Silversmith smiled. "...Remember what Miss Jane says. Trust makes for an efficient household. We need to keep asking until we find the right thing. Miss Jane is trusting us to complete her mission."

"But," Billy Dawes thought, "Finding Elizabeth Timothy in a book shop doesn't find Polly's husband, nor does it find her a home to live in. I would think that cabin is destroyed by now. Do you think Polly would return to a remote cabin to raise her baby by herself? Without ease of getting food nor water and still vulnerable to another attack?"

"Oh, I had not considered what would happen to Polly..." Silversmith replied.

"And after this mission is over?" Billy asked, "What will happen with you?"

"What do you mean, Billy?" Silversmith tilted her head uncertain how to interpret Billy's statement.

Billy continued haltingly, "What will happen to you and... me? Will your Jane Hargreaves have enough to keep me on? Or keep that butler who hired me, Witherspoon? Or can she afford to pay the rest of the Hargreaves household?" Billy Dawes looked down at his feet, "I mean, Silversmith... after this is all over will you and... I mean. Can we remain friends?"

"Oh! Oh my!" Silversmith considered, "I cannot answer for Miss Jane's ability to support more staff, but I do hope we can remain friends... I would like that very much... let us only think on being successful with our mission and allow tomorrow to worry for itself." Silversmith looked at the door of the book shop and added, "Let's go inside and inquire in a subtle manner about the whereabouts of a certain Elizabeth Timothy, shall we?"

"Subtle..." Billy echoed.

"Yes!" Silversmith stated with a bright smile, "Shall we enter the bookshop, now?"

8 CHAPTER 68: (JUNE 1776) I Bid Thee Farewell, Mr. Tweedbottom

"Are you leaving, Mr. Tweedbottom?" Jane asked as she was completing her morning sunrise stroll on the grounds of Sarah Wilson's rented Mansion.

Mr. Tweedbottom was leaning in the great front doorway of Lady Sarah Wilson's mansion watching his own luggage being loaded with difficulty by a struggling slave onto the awaiting hired carriage.

Jane stepped off the lush dew drenched grass and onto the pebble path, crunching her way toward the main entrance where Tweedbottom waited.

Jane smiled and said, "I did not see you at breakfast and I did not know you were departing from Lady Sarah Wilson's estate today."

"Hmm," Mr. Tweedbottom replied while still looking at the carriage.

Jane moved to stand boldly in front of him and said, "You don't notify me when you arrive, and you don't mention that you are leaving, Mr. Tweedbottom. Are the customs here in the colonies really that different from England? Or is your departure a hint for me to also pack my things and leave to return home?" Jane asked.

Tweedbottom now looked at her and said, "Lady Sarah Wilson said you should stay on for the remainder of the summer to help you grieve over your uncle's death."

"Grieve?" Jane started, "I did not see her ladyship at breakfast... and I have not mentioned to any person in this household that my uncle had died."

"Oh, I told her," Tweedbottom replied.

"You... took it upon yourself... Mr. Tweedbottom?" Jane asked perplexed.

"You may, " Mr. Tweedbottom uttered while looking Jane straight in the eyes, "always count on me to provide you with comfort, wisdom and solace. I informed her ladyship's guests about how I was fortunate enough to comfort you in your distressed state. I warned them of your delicate unbalanced emotions. I am heartbroken you had to endure the suffering of your Uncle's passing and wish there was something more I could do to show you my sincerity of friendship."

"My, how interesting... I am truly at a loss for words, Mr. Tweedbottom," Jane mused wondering how Mr. Tweedbottom could consider a violation of her privacy somehow a token of true friendship.

Mr. Tweedbottom continued, "I told Lady Sarah Wilson you wouldn't want to hurry back to a home where your uncle had committed self-murder and that you would accept her invitation to remain another three months."

"Accept? Three months?" Jane asked puzzled.

"It would be rude to refuse a woman of her social standing, Miss Hargreaves," Mr. Tweedbottom corrected. "She is a titled woman, after all... and you are not."

"I only wished Lady Sarah Wilson had invited me herself, but I see she trusts you, Mr. Tweedbottom, to convey such gracious niceties to me," Jane gave a small curtsy before continuing with, "A shame to see you go. Have you business elsewhere?"

"I must return to *Nieuw Amsterdam*," Mr. Tweedbottom stated.

"You mean, New York, surely," Jane smiled coyly, "Is that where you met those colorful gentlemen who have been occupying all your free time during your stay here at the estate? You always seem quite attentive to those New York gentlemen…" Jane looked around, "Have they also departed?"

Tweedbottom glanced up and down the road, mimicking Jane, and asked, "And where is your trusty Lady's Maid? I have not seen her in a while…" Tweedbottom commented, "Silversmith, was it?"

"Oh, Silversmith needs a well-deserved rest, so I sent her on. Lady Sarah Wilson has an abundance of slaves… not servants, I notice… I suppose getting wages is the only difference between the two."

"Well, slaves are a commodity to sell and trade, while servants actually study a craft, apprentice and aspire to that professional position." Tweedbottom blurted out like a parrot, "Sarah Wilson finds slaves easier to manage. Do the task or get beaten. Very simple."

"Oh? We've never discussed such matters as slavery... you and I..." Jane replied with a quizzical look. There was a silence as Tweedbottom looked down at the ground, thinking.

Tweedbottom suddenly said, "There really is only so much one can do to a gentleman's jacket, you know. I must learn to create a costume comfortable enough to be worn as their main coat, yet entrancing enough to entertain the eye. Having a creative brain is the burden men must carry."

"I liked the new red velvet jacket, which you wore when that opera fellow sang," Jane commented with a smile, "bright colors are so captivating. Are you noticing your customers at the shop are buying more brightly colored fabrics?"

"Yes, Miss, Hargreaves," Tweedbottom answered curtly as he took a step toward the carriage.

The slaves loading his items completed their task and vanished quickly.

Only the hired driver was perched atop the carriage, awaiting orders.

Mr. Tweedbottom then turned to Jane, took her hand in his and said, "I understand you require the comforts of a man such as myself, a gentleman, but even in the busy city of *Nieuw Amsterdam...* well it was New York until 1673, then back to *Nieuw Orange...* as with the Dutch prince of Orange who became King William of England... As I was saying, In *New Orange...*"

Jane interrupted, "I believe the Treaty of Westminster in 1674 required the Dutch to peaceably return the territory to Britain..."

"Right..." Tweedbottom mused, "They flew the Union Jack flag of Britain and changed Orange back to York... so, as I was saying, in New York, I found no other gentleman save myself. I quite sympathize with your loss because of me leaving the estate today."

"Pardon me?" Jane asked.

Mr. Tweedbottom replied, "I found little to converse about in that big city. I found their entertainments quite dull."

"Do the men from... um... New York... also lack modesty and humility?" Jane asked with a sudden breath of astonishment as to how any man could openly boast about being a humble, disciplined gentleman.

"Yes. Indeed they do," Mr. Tweedbottom replied with clear-eyed sincerity, "In New York, they speak loudly, fast and all at once."

"Indeed?" Jane inhaled with incredulous wide eyes.

Tweedbottom affirmed his impressions of residents of New York, "If they ask you a question, before you can utter any sort of answer, they will break out upon you again and talk, talk, talk away! They all should learn common courtesy and manners, but they are incapable of it, I fear."

"Is that why you kept company with the men, here at Sarah Wilson's estate? To teach them appropriate manners?" Jane asked, "I assumed they were from New York."

"Oh, those fellows are not from New York..." Mr. Tweedbottom paused, "They are... potential customers."

Mr. Tweedbottom turned away from Jane and stood before the door awaiting the carriage driver to lay down a step for him to ascend into the carriage, but the driver remained stony faced and up on his perch looking forward, holding the horses reins and ignoring Mr. Tweedbottom. With a snort of disgust, Mr. Tweedbottom opened his own carriage door and clumsily hauled himself up inside.

"Ah," Jane continued as Mr. Tweedbottom situated himself in the cabin and required Jane's assistance to push the door shut.

Jane prodded, "So in New York, would you have enticed an important man such as Benjamin Franklin into becoming one of your clients?"

Tweedbottom got very quiet as he stretched his arm out, trying to grasp at the door, but Jane pushed it shut unusually slowly. As he sat with pillows plumped just so, it was difficult for him to reach out and touch the door. He did not want to disturb the perfect arrangement of down-filled cushions. His fingers wiggled in the air as he waited for the door to come within his reach.

Impatiently, Mr. Tweedbottom stated, "Women don't possess the stuff to understand commerce. It is quite vulgar that you even try. A lady must know where she shines. Glow in a new gown instead of attempting to invoke names of men you will never meet. Quite irresponsible. Annoying."

He evaluated Jane's simple attire by looking at her from toe to head and then looked away with a sniff.

"Safe travels, my friend," Jane forced a smile, as she finally closed the door, took a step backwards, and saw Mr. Tweedbottom thump on the roof of the carriage to indicate the driver should commence their journey. Jane waved and spoke conversationally, knowing Mr. Tweedbottom could not hear her and said, "I bid thee fare-well, Mr. Tweedbottom."

Just as the carriage was pulling away, a slave approached and bowed to Jane before awkwardly pushing a paper at her, waiting for her to take it. Jane was more used to a well-dressed servant presenting a note on a tray, but this was the Wilson Estate and things were not as polished as Jane was used to.

Jane accepted the note and thanked the slave as he dashed away without a word. Carefully, Jane unfolded the note.

9 CHAPTER 69: (JUNE 1776) In the Meeting Town Bookshop

Silversmith and Billy Dawes entered the large bookshop in Meeting Town. The book shelves were built close together and over crowded with books and pamphlets. Customers stood scattered about engulfed in texts. Silversmith presumed that the patron over there, a woman immersed in her tiny book, was dreaming about a lover with a poetic tongue. That boy over on the other side of the bookshop was thirsting for adventure based on what he was reading. That gentleman moving slowly along another aisle seemed as if he were a researcher of sorts as he was studying and comparing texts. Silversmith and Mr. Billy Dawes couldn't tell who was the book shop manager until one gentleman walked up to another and proffered a coin for a cook book.

The shop keeper smiled, deposited the coin in a cash box, walked to a desk, wrapped the book in paper and string, then handed the parcel to the man and bade him a good day.

Silversmith and Billy quietly looked around.

"There appears to be a small sign there, on that bookshelf. Look..." Silversmith whispered and grabbed Billy Dawes' arm with anticipation. Billy secretly hoped there would be more signs in this Shoppe, which would prompt Silversmith to again grab and hold onto his arm. He swung his gaze around to spy out more items to investigate.

"There is another sign, Silversmith," Billy started... "It says Mrs. Elizabeth Timothy's works. Where her works be, perhaps she shall also be?"

Silversmith read the small words, "South Carolina Gazette newspaper owner permits this Shoppe, for a short while, to sell works she herself has penned."

"I would say," Billy shared quietly, "That they are encouraging the sale of these works by imposing a deadline after which the works will no longer be available."

Silversmith protested, "But, I do not see a woman around here who claims ownership of this shelf of books."

The shelf contained pocket sized Bibles along with other printed booklets of Mrs. Timothy's musings.

"Perhaps," Billy Dawes started, "She was successful with selling her books in her colony and is seeing if they will sell in another colony."

"Perhaps," Silversmith concurred.

Without warning, Billy Dawes abruptly reached over to a bookshelf, swiped a small book, then took two steps to the shopkeeper's counter.

"I'd like to purchase this fine book," Billy said loudly while slapping a coin on the counter, right on top of the bound volume. "I've heard the author is a fine woman of wisdom and her thoughts captured on these pages are better than gold. What do you know of this Elizabeth Timothy?"

Silversmith was embarrassed at Billy's sudden and loud tactics. She sidled up to him indicating that he can speak a bit more softly.

"Have you indeed heard such things?" A gentleman customer cooed as he turned toward Billy and Silversmith.

"Yes. Sir," Billy replied, now realizing

he should have looked at the title of the book, but he was here to engage in conversation so he turned to the man and asked, "Have you read the works of Elizabeth Timothy?"

"Indeed I have, as I am Mrs. Timothy's son, Peter." The gentleman smiled, "but if you look at that particular book, you'll see it is by 'anonymous.'"

"But," Billy stammered as he now noticed the author was indeed anonymous, "...it was on the shelf of works by Elizabeth Timothy."

"Oh," the man replied, "It is authored by Elizabeth Timothy. But it does not say it because of the subject of the book."

"I do not understand," Silversmith interjected.

The man smiled, "Elizabeth Timothy's husband started the Gazette and after he died, she continued the business. She became close friends with the investor's wife, Deborah Read Franklin. I still treasure the Bible she gave us long ago."

"Franklin?" Silversmith repeated with a note of excitement.

"Yes," the man replied, "Benjamin Franklin." He paused, then added, "Mr. Franklin invested in the paper and for the sake of a lady's reputation, he suggested it be printed as anonymous, but in fact it is the combined wisdom of Widow Timothy and Mrs. Franklin."

"Indeed!" Silversmith announced.

"How do you know these details, Sir?" Billy Dawes prodded.

The man replied, "As I've just said, I am Mrs. Elizabeth Timothy's son, Peter Timothy. I am travelling about to encourage book sellers to promote my mother's works. They are quite good, you see."

"Is your mother nearby?" Silversmith asked.

The shop keeper dropped Billy Dawes' coin into his cash box and started to wrap the book in paper and string.

It was then that Silversmith and Billy noticed the title of the book was "Reflections on Courtship and Marriage."

The man who introduced himself as Peter Timothy shared, "My mother died, back in 1757. I still recall when she would sell books from our home, which was right next to the Gazette's printing office. The best Whig newspaper around…" Peter Timothy became lost in thought for a moment.

"Did I hear you correctly that your mother died in 1757? Nearly twenty years ago?" Silversmith clarified, then muttered to herself, "I suppose she isn't in town visiting, then." She looked down despondent.

Peter Timothy replied, "My father was not the best at managing business accounts. I was her seventh child, you see. Mr. Benjamin Franklin saw my mother was organized and possessed that diligent Dutch work ethic. Mr. Franklin continued to invest in the newspaper and discovered my mother was a better manager than my father was. She grew the business. When she died, she left me the Gazette along with a silver watch. I hope to continue the newspaper's success. I hope my own children will continue the business after I die."

"All the inheritance went to the youngest?" Billy Dawes asked clumsily. Silversmith blushed at such a direct question.

Peter Timothy laughed it off, "Very direct, my good sir. No. My mother left my sisters slaves and property... in abundance. They had interests besides publishing."

Billy Dawes asked, "So, your mother sold newspapers and books?"

Peter replied, "She sold more than just the news. My mother published:

Testaments, Confessions of Faith with Notes, Virtue Rewarded, Dyche's spelling books, Westminster Confessions of Faith, Cato on Old Age, Familiar Instructor, Allen's Alarm and Dr. Armstrong's Poems on Health, Watt's Devine Songs... Oh, I love his music as much as his Psalms and Hymns, Don't you?"

"Indeed we do, Sir!" Silversmith stated

Billy Dawes leaned over to Silversmith, "Who is Watt?" he whispered, but she ignored his question.

The shopkeeper pushed the wrapped volume to Billy Dawes with a, "Thank you very much, Sir" he then moved off to assist another customer.

Peter Timothy leaned over to Billy Dawes with a smile and said, "Some assumed that since Benjamin Franklin was the investor in the Gazette that he wrote the book you hold there, but I assure you it was written by a woman. If you wish to decipher the mind of a woman, inside those pages is advice I myself employed with my wife very happily."

"I see," Billy said as he started to open the paper the book was wrapped in to peek inside the pages a bit, "This was a most serendipitous purchase, then."

"So," Silversmith added, "If my mistress wanted to meet Mr. Franklin, are you able to foster an introduction?"

Peter Timothy shared, "Well, he has become occupied by more political affairs of late. So, I am not quite on familiar terms with him... but you both seem to be amiable... And admirers of my mother's works when there are so many other authors from which to select in this shop."

"Yes?" Silversmith asked with anticipation.

Opening to a random page from the book he had just purchased, Billy Dawes read aloud, "...Unhappy matches are often occasioned by mercenary views in one or both parties... ill conducted passion... uh,"

He skipped down the page and continued, "abominable protestations of persons and minds are daily seen in many of our marriages! So few truly share real friendship and esteem... How many play the aggrieved for a good settlement under the legal title of wife. How many men are stallions to repair a broken fortune... he finds by experience he fell in Love with his own Ideas, and she with her own Vanity." Billy looked up.

"Oh, read on," Peter Timothy urged.

Billy Dawes cleared his throat, "The real felicity of marriage consists of union of minds, sympathy of affection, mutual esteem for each other. Unhappy marriages are from the headstrong motives of ungoverned passions..."

"What is meant by that?" Billy asked Peter.

Peter Timothy replied, "My mother and

Deborah Franklin would discuss relationships. She would oft times tell me that if I based my selection of a wife only on physical passions, my future marriage would be doomed."

He smiled to himself as if listening to a conversation from his past, recalling the wisdom shared with him. He inhaled, then continued, "If, however, I considered her character to determine if her values would be like mine, and if we could count on each other in difficult times, then we could build something together, respect each other, then we would have very few difficulties indeed... and the passion would be just as fulfilling... and she was proven right."

Peter looked at Billy Dawes, "...but as I mentioned earlier... this is not exactly a volume on botany. It is a subject unsuitable for a respectable widow and mother of seven children to discuss, let alone publish and sell."

Billy summarized, "So, women are taught to incite the passions of men..."

Silversmith gave Billy Dawes an angry look then turned to Peter and said, "Mr. Timothy. Would you be able to introduce my mistress to..."

Billy interrupted, "Please call me Billy, Mr. Timothy."

"And you," Peter Timothy replied, "call me Peter. So, yes. It is a fascinating topic to discuss..."

"Could you expound on your point, Sir?" Billy asked.

"In our modern world, here in the colonies," Peter stated, "most men will enter the contract of marriage either based solely on passions, or upon the promise of increased fortune. Those marriages die and both husband and wife take on... perhaps other unfortunate arrangements. Yet, the marriages based on respect, character, loyalty also get the passions, but not until sometime after the wedding. Those are the ones which last and are nourishing to your soul."

Billy interjected, "Many of my friends have married an empty headed, yet enthusiastic woman. One to pass the evening hours with amongst friends and beer."

"And," Peter continued, "Once the lure of an empty-headed wife fades, no matter how beautiful or social she is, a man is left hungry to exchange ideas and this is why he seeks a mistress."

Peter cleared his throat to observe how his words impacted his audience, Billy Dawes and Silversmith.

Billy raised his brow in surprise, and Silversmith frowned.

Cautiously, Peter Timothy continued to clarify, "My mother's education saved our family newspaper, and made her attractive to many men... though she was proudly loyal to her husband, my father. Her insights allowed all seven of us to make good marriages. My mother could converse on nearly any subject. Eventually, I married an intelligent woman who could also converse and it has kept our love alight."

Peter Timothy looked at Billy Dawes and Silversmith and smiled, "Perhaps you both would enjoy reading poetry together, to bask in the romance of words..."

Billy Dawes cleared his throat and avoided eye contact while tucking the book inside his jacket pocket.

"I admire the directness of both of you," Peter Timothy laughed as he guided them out of the shop, "and I am pleased my mother's wisdom will help your... uh... friendship progress..." He turned to Silversmith and said, "I have not forgotten your request about introducing your mistress to Mr. Benjamin Franklin."

Peter smiled again.

"It was quite rude of me to have ignored you earlier, but I was lured in by a topic I do not normally have the luxury of exploring. To pay for my social injury done to you, Miss, may I offer you information as to where Mr. Franklin will be gathering with others to discuss the affairs of our Colonies?"

"Oh?" Silversmith now felt rejuvenated, "I do accept that meeting location as an apt apology, Mr. Timothy." Silversmith grinned broadly.

Peter continued, "I cannot introduce you directly to Mr. Franklin as it has been some time since I last saw him, however there is a woman who can make an introduction on your behalf if she feels it prudent."

"A woman?" Billy Dawes replied, "An empty-headed vision of beauty?".

"Not one as lovely as your current companion," Peter smiled as they stood in the dusty street outside the bookshop, "But a very wise and interesting woman. I happen to know where the next meeting will be where both Susanna Wright and Benjamin Franklin will hopefully be discussing issues I care about."

"Susanna Wright?" Silversmith asked to clarify, "...could introduce my mistress to Ambassador Benjamin Franklin?"

"I guarantee nothing," Peter smiled, "But would be happy to take you as far as I can. The rest will be for you to decide."

"Billy Dawes turned to Silversmith and quietly whispered in her ear, "Oh, now I know what you meant by 'subtle'."

10 What Just Happened?

While Jane is sleuthing for justice, Bryce Aiden Tyler discusses a theory with the Magistrate pertaining to how he thinks Uncle Floyd was killed.

Meanwhile, Polly learned about the secret of her host, Mrs. Dunlap.

Jane is forming her assumptions about Mr. Tweedbottom, and now wonders if cultivating him as a romantic prospect is wise or not. Jane wants to make sure any man she is entangled with in a bond of matrimony has a very strong ethical character. Is Mr. Tweedbottom such a prospect? Or not?

Meanwhile, Silversmith and Billy Dawes progress in their investigations of these secret meetings where great minds gather to try and establish the course of these colonies in this strange new untamed land. But, will they succeed in gaining access to the elusive Ambassador Franklin?

11 Did You Know...

Opera was popular in France and Italy before the 1600's. Some felt this form of entertainment clashed with ballet, which was popular among the European elite.

Pomone (1671) is sometimes referred to as the first French opera. It included ballet and other visually appealing staging. The performance established the *Académie Royale de Musique* (now the Paris Opéra) on March 3, 1671. *Castor et Pollux* (1737; libretto by Pierre-Joseph-Justin Bernard), a tragédie that was performed at the Paris Opéra 254 times in 48 years.

In England, however, opera was not popular. Instead, the "court masque" was a form of entertainment based on ballet and fancied by royals of the 16th and 17th centuries. These were poetic works which focused on subjects of allegory and myth, displayed on stage with dancing, acting, and singing. Additionally, mid-century civil wars, which hurt the local economy, did not provide an environment to nurture the arts. .

Some early operas in England were composed for private audiences, not public theaters. It is thought that among these early operas for private performance were *Venus and Adonis* (about 1683) by John Blow, along with *Dido and Aeneas* (about 1689) by Henry Purcell.

Some believe England did not actively develop operas for public theaters until the 19th century.

German composer George Frideric Handel apprenticed in Italy, then moved to London in 1710. His opera company soon became very popular for the next three decades by producing Neapolitan opera. His unique style of harmony, melody and drama makes his works memorable even today. But, as fashion and tastes in entertainment moved away from Italian style opera, Handel started having financial difficulties. He focused on producing works which catered to the Protestant middle-class. These included oratorios; set to Biblical texts in English, which could be sung by a solo artist, or a choir of voices, and accompanied by an orchestra.

So the artistic tastes of Royalty, and what they chose to financially support, influenced the culture of the nation. On the 17th of July 1717, King George I arranged for a concert on the Thames River where a barge floated, and from which 50 musicians serenaded him performing Handel's *Water Music.* As his majesty floated upstream to Chelsea and then returned to Whitehall, the musicians replayed Handel's music three times.

An aspect which may have contributed to Handle's works losing favor with the public was the introduction of the London production of the 1728 *The Beggar's Opera* which was arranged by Johann Christoph Pepusch, with a libretto by John Gay. Here, characters were presented as crude and bawdy. The production itself mocked traditional opera. This was a form of entertainment which could be understood by all social classes. *The Beggar's Opera* soon traveled throughout the British Isles.

The work "Hallelujah" is from the *Messiah*, a 260-page oratorio. Handle started working on this on August 22, 1741, and completed the composition in 24 days on September 14, 1741.

Some believe that King George I adored opera performances. It is estimated during the 1726-1727 season, his Majesty saw Handel's *Admeto* 19 times, attended various concerts, and paid a £1,000 subscription to the Royal Academy of Music.

12 Vocabulary

In the early 1770s, before the colonies united into the United States of America, some words and terms were used, which may be explained in this section.

Coffers: A strong box for saving money or valuables, such as jewelry.

Distraught : Upset and worried so you cannot think clearly.

Foppish   (Page 75) Originally used around the 1600's, this term described a man who is foolishly obsessed with how he appears, concerned more with shoe-buckles and lace-cuffs and taking a substance to make him feel elated, focusing only on his own comforts rather than upon matters which would impact those around him. ...

Foyer: Just inside the main door,the foyer is a room which leads to the rest of the house.

Interject: To throw other things in between. To interrupt while another person is still speaking.

mandated: A formal order from a higher official to act or speak in a certain way.

succinct: Clearly said in just a few words with no wasted extra words.

ABOUT Wynter Sommers

Wynter Sommers is the pseudonym for an American writing team, which harnesses multiple skills in technology, research, history and education. Formally trained with a PhD in Education, Wynter Sommers blends academic classroom experience, with corporate sophistication, and a passion for developing more effective student insights through engaging storytelling.

Wynter Sommers has a heart to inspire creativity and develop critical thinking skills, all to encourage readers to make wise choices in life.

Wynter Sommers takes each story and weaves the plot with classic gripping elements, which endure throughout repeated readings, revealing new meanings each time the story is explored. The small choices a reader makes in real life could have a lasting effect in future generations. This set of stories shows the origin of not just Bjorn Esterday and Sarah Paradise, but of their ancestors and the sort of world which was established, which unfolded in each generation until Bjorn and Sarah met.

It is rewarding to learn of heartfelt, thought provoking conversations taking place globally about the characters of these books. Should the reader be presented with extraordinary circumstances, it is the sincerest wish that they act with honor, truth and integrity to overcome obstacles in real life whilst the reader hones skills of self-reliance and collaborative teamwork despite barriers outside of the reader's control. Wynter Sommers hopes you enjoy the other *Bjorn Esterday Was not Born Yesterday* stories in this series.